DATE DUE

GAYLORD   PRINTED IN U.S.A.

The Baker's Dozen

The Baker's Dozen

DAN ANDREASEN

Henry Holt and Company ∽ New York

The baker takes great care
to make one cream éclair.

1

In the oven he bakes
two German chocolate cakes.

2

In tins the perfect size
he bakes three cherry pies.

3

The icing drips and runs
atop four sticky buns.

4

He rolls the dough and then
he cuts five cookie men.

5

With fruit from mixing bowls
he fills six jelly rolls.

6

On doilies shaped like hearts
he places seven tarts.

7

With icing he draws doodles
on top of eight warm strudels.

8

Marshmallow slowly heats
to make nine crispy treats.

9

With nuts of many sorts
he bakes ten little tortes.

10

He measures with teaspoons
eleven macaroons.

11

He knows just what it takes
to make twelve small cupcakes.

12

At last his job's complete—
now thirteen folks to greet!

13

1

2

3

4

5

6

7

8

9

10

11

12

13

For Katrina

Henry Holt and Company, LLC
Publishers since 1866
175 Fifth Avenue
New York, New York 10010
www.henryholtchildrensbooks.com

Distributed in Canada by H. B. Fenn and Company Ltd.

Library of Congress Cataloging-in-Publication Data
Andreasen, Dan.
The baker's dozen: a counting book / Dan Andreasen.—1st ed.
p.   cm.
Summary: The reader is invited to count from one to thirteen as
a jolly baker makes delectable treats from one mouth-watering éclair
to twelve luscious cupcakes, and serves them to invited guests.
ISBN-13: 978-0-8050-7809-1 / ISBN-10: 0-8050-7809-6
[1. Baking—Fiction. 2. Counting—Fiction. 3. Stories in rhyme.]
I. Title. II. Title: Counting book.
PZ8.3.A55195Bak 2007   [E]—dc22   2006031372

First Edition—2007 / Designed by Amelia May Anderson
Printed in the United States of America on acid-free paper. ∞

1 3 5 7 9 10 8 6 4 2

The artist used oil paint on gessoed illustration board
to create the illustrations for this book.